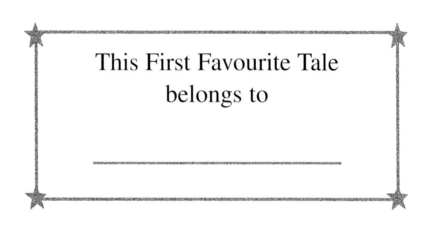

This First Favourite Tale
belongs to

BASED ON A TRADITIONAL FOLK TALE
retold by Ronne Randall ★ *illustrated by* Liz Pichon

Published by Ladybird Books Ltd
A Penguin Company
Penguin Books Ltd, 80 Strand, London WC2R 0RL, UK
Penguin Books Australia Ltd, 707 Collins Street, Melbourne, Victoria 3008, Australia
Penguin Group (NZ), 67 Apollo Drive, Rosedale, Auckland 0632, New Zealand

028

© LADYBIRD BOOKS MCMXCIX

ISBN: 978-0-72149-739-6

Printed in China

The Little Red Hen

One sunny spring morning, the little red hen was scratching about the farmyard.

Suddenly…

"Look! Look!" clucked the little red hen. "I spy…

"…an ear of corn!"

The little red hen was *very* excited! She showed it to her friends in the farmyard.

"Who will help me to plant this corn?" she asked.

"Not I," yawned the sleepy, stripey cat.

"Not I," sniffed the sleek, skinny rat.

"Not I," snorted the plump, pink pig.

"Then I will plant this corn myself," said the little red hen.

And she did.

The little red hen weeded and watered the corn every day.

Soon the corn began to grow.

It grew . . . and it grew . . .

...and it **grew** till it was tall and golden.

"Who will help me to cut the corn?" asked the little red hen.

"Not I," purred the preening, stripey cat.

"Not I," sang the snoozing, skinny rat.

"Not I," mumbled the muddy, pink pig.

Too busy!

"Then I will cut the corn myself," said the little red hen.

And she did.

"Who will help me to take this corn to the mill?" asked the little red hen.

"Not I," said the big, stripey cat.

"Not I," shouted the small, skinny rat.

"Not I," laughed the large, pink pig.

Too busy!

"Then I will take this corn to the mill myself," said the little red hen.

And she did.

Round and round went the windmill as it ground the corn.

Soon the little red hen had a big sack of fine white flour to take home.

She was *very* pleased!

"Who will help me to bake some bread?" asked the little red hen.

"Not I," called the curled-up, stripey cat.

"Not I," said the sneaky, skinny rat.

"Not I," giggled the gleeful, pink pig.

"Then I will bake the bread myself," said the little red hen.

And she did.

Mmmmm!

"Who will help me to eat this bread?"
asked the little red hen.

"I will!" said the eager, stripey cat. "It smells so-o-o delicious!"

"I will!" said the hungry, skinny rat. "I *love* freshly baked bread!"

"I will!" said the greedy, pink pig. "With lots of creamy butter, please!"

But the little red hen had other plans.

"Not you, stripey cat! Not you, skinny rat! Not you, greedy pig! You didn't help me at all. So now I'm going to eat this warm, fresh bread all by myself."

And she did… with *oodles* of creamy butter!